Im-Bruegel-io!

Adam Paxman

DEDICATIONS

For Lucy,
who first mentioned ekphrastic writing to me,
setting this compulsive poetic output in motion.

For Jo and Aisla,
who suffered through recitals in the office.

Dear souls, all.

CONTENTS

ACKNOWLEDGMENTS

This anthology would not have been possible without
the sterling work of Pieter Bruegel the Elder.
If reading these silly poems
makes one person look at
his paintings anew,
job done.

I also Googled some stuff.

EXPOSITORY NOTE

It probably helps to know that Lucy and Adam are teachers. Busy scuttling creatures, teachers must scavenge for amusement where they can find it. Recently, Lucy came across the word ekphrastic in a webinar synopsis. Being a logophile and quick to bristle at unnecessarily convoluted academic terminology, Adam immediately looked up the term ekphrasis online. Soon both Lucy and Adam were tickled pink by ekphrastic poetry.

Ekphrastic writing traditionally takes a work of visual art – real or imagined - and renders it in rhetorical prose or poetry, in order to uncover obscure narrative and/or semantic associations, or to invent ambiguous new contexts. Here, Pieter Bruegel (or Brueghel) the Elder's 1562 oil painting on oak panel *Two Monkeys*, already an enduring conundrum, was the inspiration for Lucy and Adam's haiku poems, which were fired back and forth over Facebook Messenger one night after work.

Haiku turned out to be a bit of a sloppy misnomer. Apparently, the commonly held syllable count of Japanese haiku; five-seven-five, or seventeen total; was used to teach school children the form. Thematically, haiku is conventionally attached to moments, insights into human nature, and seasonal or natural themes, and generally includes several standard linguistic devices – a seasonal word, or kigo, for instance. In terms of metre and rhythm, Japanese kana differ significantly from English syllables, therefore Lucy and Adam were ignorantly adopting the foreign form without any regard for the theme or genre of a haiku. Another type of Japanese poetry, senryū, similarly feature the five-seven-five syllable structure, but tends to be more cynical, focusing on the fallibility or emotional states of human beings in darkly humorous ways. Lucy and Adam used an elastic synthesis of these poetic forms, with either three-five-three or five-seven-five syllables, to respond to Bruegel's painting.

For the remaining poems in this anthology, Adam kept the seventeen syllable senryū form, though in some instances utilised this as a verse structure, to craft unexpected longer form narratives.

EKPHRASTIC MONKEYS

It's my turn

now to watch the boats.

Please turn round.

To break these

bonds we will need a

large chisel.

Remember

rainforest freedom!

don't give up.

Feel shame,

chained monkeys two.

Feel ashamed.

No sailing,

you naughty monkeys.

Just sit still.

The monkey

to my left always

makes a mess.

Sail away.

Leave the two monkeys

behind us.

Bananas.

I crave bananas.

No more nuts.

How do I

break it to her I

have the key?

Got filler?

that Brueghel fella

etched his name.

Help! Help! Help!

We are trapped in an

old painting.

Get these chains off first,

then lure those ducks with nuts and

fly off on their backs.

Double glazing would

vastly improve energy

efficiency, right?

There has to be a

better way to pulverise

walnuts into flour.

Zoo cutbacks

blamed for small monkey

enclosures.

Please look away.

I cannot pee if you are

watching me.

We have ten too few

monkeys to remake the film

Twelve Monkeys.

Years from now

they'll fire our children

into orbit.

THE MISANTHROPE (1568)

I.

You gotta pick a

pocket or two; gotta pick

a pocket or two.

Is that a hay bale

on your back? What's with the cross?

A Christian bale?

Accursed pudding
or big ball of dung, what's with

the naughty thieving?

Or are you an orb

representing God's millstone

dragging down peasants?

Why you pilfering

that guy's kidney? To transplant

or bake in a pud?

Oh, it's a coin purse!

No organ harvesting here -

you are just a crook.

What you gonna buy
with all those ill-gotten gains?

A pair of new shoes?

Your trendy leggings

are ripped at the knee –

cyclical fashion.

That sinister man

could be part of a police

sting operation.

II.

You are a bent tree.

Was it windy as you grew?

That's a nasty split.

I suppose that you
could be home to animals —

An owl, bat, woodworms.

III.

You are two mushrooms.

Large ruddy or brown caps and

white stems visible.

I cannot make out

your bulbous volva, ring or

scales — best not eat you.

The flat, dusty field

is no place to deposit

reproductive spores.

IV.

Mind those caltrops, you!

Even in those nice black shoes

you'll feel quite a prick.

Where are you going?

And where have you been? Frozen

in place and space/time.

What are you planning

to spend all your hard-earned dosh

on? Sheep? Toys? Gifts? Sweets?

Tobacco? Sugar?

A new spring/summer season

cloak in garish hues?

You probably have

a very good reason to

be stern or upset.

Life is hard enough

without the added drama

of muggers, caltrops.

What are you hiding

under that cloak? Dwarfs stacked on

each other's shoulders?

V.

Farmer, tend your sheep.

As they are black and white, you

can play chess with them.

You are far away

from the mugging taking place

on the dusty path.

What's that implement?

From here it looks like you are

practicing putting.

VI.

Windmill, turn your sails -

generate green energy

or grind some grain.

VII.

Ruminating sheep,

chew your cud – for digestion

requires you do.

VIII.

The medium is

ironic – distemper for

a sombre old soul.

AND YOLK WITH A STRAW:

An ekphrastic poem inspired by

Pieter Bruegel the Elder's

The Beekeepers and the Birdnester (1568)

I.

Oi! Oi! You! Yes, you!

Whatever are you doing,

hugging that tree branch?

Are you trying to

stop it being torn down and

used for firewood?

Or halt construction

of a new road or bypass

or housing estate?

Or are you just a

tree hugger? You know, someone

in touch with nature.

What species of tree

is that? Do you know? I have

no idea at all.

I'd have to consult

a reference book or ask

a dendrologist.

Are you scrumping for

apples, pears or other fruit?

Is it a fruit tree?

Or rather are you

hiding from eerie masked men

by climbing that tree?

Oh, sorry, yes, shush.

You clearly are hiding from

them. I'll be quiet.

II.

Who or what are they?

they have no faces at all -

it's creepy as fuck.

Are they even real?

They could be apparitions.

You know, like spirits.

But what would ghosts want

with all those wicker baskets?

Redecorating?

If storage space is

at a premium, they come

in very handy.

You can stow hand soaps,

liquid soap dispensers and

flannels, shaving foam,

razors, tweezers, gel.

Any toiletries, really.

Towels, nail clippers.

The ghosts may well be

Minimalists – all white walls,

a clean, sterile space.

No clutter, no shelves,

no French dressers, bric-a-brac,

collectible plates.

I guess a white space

could be advantageous for

spirits to hide in.

Oh, they're wearing masks!

Why didn't you say something?

Letting me blather

on and on about

spirits and all that other

hokum. So silly!

They are probably

in a weird folksy cult.

Like *The Wicker Man.*

Not Alan Whicker.

I mean the film remake with

Nicolas Cage in.

III.

Beekeepers, you say?

So, all those wicker baskets

are really beehives?

I think I would wear

protective gloves if I were

around bees all day.

I mean, beestings are

decidedly unpleasant.

Full robes but no gloves!

I suppose honey

was more important in the

sixteenth century.

Refining sugar

was not mastered for very

many centuries.

Honey was a cheap,

natural way to sweeten

food – and delicious.

That would make it worth

a few stings on bare, exposed

hands. A few deaths too.

Human life is cheap.

Peasant life even more so.

Existential, eh?

IV.

Well, going back to

my original question:

Why are you up there?

Did you forget your

robe and mask today? Are you

an apiarist?

Are you scared of bees?

Allergic? Don't want to get

stung? They can fly though.

A tree's a bad spot

to hide from a swarm of bees.

They may sting your bum.

Once in school, my friend

sat on a bee at playtime -

it looked quite painful.

I heard that modern

beekeepers use smoke to make

The bees feel drowsy.

Maybe light a fag.

Or a pipe, cigar or one

of them vape thingies.

You could set the tree

on fire, but then you might

get set on fire.

V.

You're stealing bird eggs?

I believe the practice was

common in the past.

It's been illegal

for over a hundred years.

Birdnesting, it's called.

It is also known

As egging – the collection

of pretty bird eggs.

You can arrange them

by size or colouration.

What's the other term?

Oology, right?

You blow out the albumen

and yolk with a straw.

Why do you do it?

I mean, why does anyone

collect anything?

What I'm asking is,

are you a collector; or

are you just hungry?

Nowadays you can

have a dozen free range eggs

dropped on the doorstep.

Not hard enough to

crack them – that would be no good!

In a sturdy box.

All it takes is a

few clicks of a computer

mouse, phone or tablet.

Alternatively,

you can buy eggs from the shops

or supermarket.

Chicken eggs, I mean.

Do you like eating bird eggs?

I've eaten quail eggs.

They were nice but small.

You need a few to get full.

Quails nest on the ground.

So, I suppose that

you can't be after quail eggs.

What eggs are they then?

Are they blue tit eggs?

Sparrow? Goldfinch? Long-tailed tit?

Are they even nice?

Do you eat them raw?

Or do you poach them? Fry them?

Scramble them? Coddle?

It's not about taste.

It's the environmental

impact of poaching.

Stealing eggs, I mean.

Not cooking them in water.

Poaching eggs is bad.

The reason why we

don't eat or collect bird eggs

is conservation.

Hen eggs are farmed on

a vast industrial scale –

hens aren't endangered.

I assume you are

from the peasant class due to

outward appearance.

Perhaps you are a

bored provincial landowner,

become eccentric.

Are you desperate?

Out of work? Injured? Poorly?

Too poor to buy eggs?

I'm not judging you.

Socioeconomic

pressures lead to crime.

I'm sure you pilfer

wild bird eggs only because

you have no options.

There's no reason to

assume that all peasants are

rascals and varmints.

On the other hand,

if it *is* a snack you need,

try a ham sandwich.

FIFTEEN SIXTY-TWO

Ekphrastic poems

turn non-literary art

into poetry.

Senryu poems

use a syllabic pattern

of five-seven-five.

Senryu poems

focus on human nature,

satire, dark humour.

The Triumph of Death (1562)

The Triumph of Death

is one heck of a painting.

You should Google it.

This saturnine scene

is as relevant now as

when it was painted.

Death as conqueror,

common denominator,

inevitable.

It could represent

today's global pandemic,

historical plagues.

It's like Saturday

night in town after payday –

absolute carnage.

The swimmer (top left):

"If I just hang around here

they may not see me."

"Even with all the

skeletons drowning people

I feel safer here."

Seated skeleton

considers a bird carcass.

A doubtful soldier?

Seated skeleton

too near skeletons with horns?

Or just hungover?

Clustered skeletons

with vuvuzelas; is this

a spectator sport?

Emaciated

dog is sniffing or eating

a tiny baby.

Bad dog! Stop it now!

Leave that poor little baby.

Things are bleak enough.

Skeletons in red

robes and fetching hoods pull a

coffin on blue wheels.

The wheels will get stuck

on the occupant's husband;

his corpse is beneath.

At the bottom right,

two lovers are ignorant

of their destiny.

They must both be quite

short-sighted not to notice

pandemonium.

Elsewhere, a flayed horse

tramples over stampeding

humans, which would hurt.

The skinless horsey's

rider is a skeleton

waving a big scythe.

I wonder what thoughts

are going through its head now?

What crazy farming.

The skeletons are

in different stages of

decay, but all smiles.

The king's time is up.

A helpful skeleton holds

an hourglass up.

Wristwatches had yet

to be invented - telling

time would have been hard.

Barrels full of gold

and silver coins scattered

across the bare earth.

A skeleton digs

bony hands in the coffers;

a futile fortune.

The dinner table

is in disarray; bread rolls,

skulls — what a menu!

Peasants cower neath

a wagon of skulls, drawn by

a pale, sickly horse.

Grasping pitchforks they

must know it's a terrible

place in which to hide.

Can there really be

such a high demand for skulls?

Where do they sell them?

The poorly thin horse

would benefit from someone

brushing its lank mane.

Fiery Hell cart,

what is thy purpose? Toasting

captive birds to eat?

I suppose it's good

the skeleton army brings

its own catering.

Hitting skeletons

with swords - this will not end well.

Make a run for it!

Skeleton army

is overwhelming in its

thronging multitudes.

Men of every

creed and class are captured

in a net and drowned.

Is that a giant

coffin that they are being

herded into? Yes.

Another bloodless

massacre – was censorship

much stricter back then?

At least most of the

skeletons look like they are

having a nice time.

The Fall of the Rebel Angels (1562)

That same year,

Bruegel painted *The Fall of*

the Rebel Angels.

It was inspired

by the battle for Heaven

in Revelation.

The oil on panel

painting, misattributed

to Bruegel's own son,

As well as fellow

Dutchman Hieronymus Bosch,

depicts Satan's fall.

Let's ekphrasticise!

What new interpretations

will we discover?

I.

A flying goose

with plucked body is firing

or dropping an egg.

Is goose passing by

or is she involved in this

absolute shit-storm?

Rebel angels are

transformed into animals

as they fall from grace.

A large green lobster

with mussels for wings chases

mosquito people.

They're on the same side,

aren't they? Maybe they're tumbling

or just want a chat.

II.

This Heavenly war

takes place before the whole snake,

Eve, fruit fiasco.

That's why the serpent

still has limbs; they're not cut off

until *Genesis*.

III.

It's a goddamn shame,

the weather in Heaven looks

really quite pleasant.

The rebels will be

cast out unto wet blue Earth,

or the inferno.

I wonder what it's

like in Heaven. Changeable

climate and seasons?

Does Heaven ever

suffer droughts? Are there monsoons?

Mudslides? Tsunamis?

Or is the weather

eternally consistent

like Los Angeles?

Presumably the

Pit is always very warm.

No radiators.

When they all get there

I imagine Hell will be

just an empty cave.

A fixer-upper.

Would it actually be

Hell before they come?

Or will they bring all

the fixtures and fittings with

them from Paradise?

This begs the question:

why would Heavenly angels

have tools for torture?

They have the fire

to forge weapons like Vulcan.

Lots and lots of flames.

It's renewable

geothermal energy.

Is the Devil green?

I digress. God knows

if Hell is unionised

or heat efficient.

IV.

So, for now they fall,

assuming their strange new forms –

frogs, fish and monsters.

Michael's angels blow

long curved trumpets – are angels

scared by loud noises?

Is a victory

fanfare a touch premature?

Toot, toot, toot, toot, toot.

It's a crazy jazz,

a truly cacophonic

din to drive them out.

Some of God's angels

smite them with swords; a bloodless,

chaotic maelstrom.

V.

The great red dragon -

seven crowned heads -

from *Apocalypse*.

A prophecy of

The end times tangled up with

Satan's origin.

Time is out of joint,

the beginning and the end

simultaneous.

That naked demon's

breastplate sundial must not work;

an ouroboros.

Time-keeping must be

tough in Heaven – appraisal

targets confounding.

Naturalia

and *artificialia*

are here intertwined.

The demon's turban,

knife and crown of thorns,

screaming moth torso,

armadillo plates,

plant stems bursting from bodies,

cabbage heads, fur gloves,

an Ottoman helm

easily mistaken for

a lemon squeezer,

twig egg wasp stinger

hermit bird, caesarean

frog releasing spawn,

insects, skeletal

mammals, crustaceans and a

blown up pufferfish,

beasts with scaled armour

and exposed farting bum holes -

column of disgrace.

What more can I say?

Pride comes before a fall seems

far too obvious.

OUR SCHOOL MULE

I

I've heard of hamsters,
gerbils, rabbits, guinea pigs
and mice as class pets.

In my infant school,
kids had to take it in turns
to care for the pet

over summer breaks.
The class rodent was at my
friend's house when it died.

His mum put it in
the freezer so that it could
have a funeral

when the autumn term
began – probably also
to cover her back.

But a school donkey?
You couldn't get a whole ass
in your chest freezer.

You would have to chop
it up into smaller bits,
label them with care.

School mule disposal
is probably quite tricky.
Wait for Bonfire Night?

If cremating a
large class pet, do you save the
ashes to grit with?

Do glue factories
use asses, or just horses?
Is burial best?

Who digs the big hole?
The caretaker? Or should it
be a class project?

II
The moral of this
piece is not everyone can
be educated.

Having worked as a
lecturer, my feelings are
mixed on the topic.

The idea that
an ass cannot become a
horse is different

to peasant children
being taught to read and write
to better themselves.

Bruegel must not have
heard of inclusive for all
education, or

state education,
disability support,
polytechnics, or

comprehensive schools,
colleges with widening
participation

students. He may not
have ever dreamed of a time
of equality

of learning experience.
School must have changed a lot since
fifteen fifty-six.

III
Our school mule is great.
He sings to us from hymn sheets –
a devout donkey.

Our school mule is neat.
He clears up after us when
the school day is through.

Our school mule is smart.
He corrects the teacher's sums
and also, spellings.

Our school mule is quick,
he beat the rival school mule
(a donkey derby).

Our school mule plays games.
His favourite is Pin the
Tail on the Donkey.

Our school mule runs the
tuck shop from his stable door
during our playtimes.

Our school mule is
an outsider looking in.
Have you felt that way?

Our school mule conducts
teaching observations to
ensure high standards.

Our school mule canes us
during assembly and gives
tedious sermons.

Our school mule only
reads us stories with donkeys
and asses in them.

Our school mule makes chips
and greasy pizzas. He is
our dinner lady.

Our school mule makes the
thickest lumpy gravy and
pale yellow custard.

Our school mule is on
a zero hours' contract, he'd
better watch his ass.

Our school mule never,
ever uses mouthwash - those
mouthwash adverts lie.

Our school mule is fed
sausages that hang from the
classroom letterbox.

Our school mule is dead.
We have no chest freezer, so
our school mule is meat.

ABOUT THE AUTHOR

Adam Paxman was born and raised in a small village just outside the historic walled city of York. In secondary school, he entered an essay writing competition, the brief for which was to celebrate the brewery town of Tadcaster. Despite having entered a sarcastic, satirical and scatological poem, Adam won third prize. After an awards luncheon, Adam was struck down with food poisoning, as the caterers had left cooked chicken drumsticks in direct sunlight. It took several decades for Adam to build up the courage to once again write poems.

Adam's first collection of sarcastic, satirical and scatological illustrated short stories, *Misanthropology*, is available from Amazon.

Printed in Great Britain
by Amazon